W9-BEH-585

# Reading
# *The Giver*

THE ENGAGED READER

Reading *The Giver*

Reading *The Adventures of Tom Sawyer*

Reading *Johnny Tremain*

Reading *The Diary of Anne Frank*

Reading *Sounder*

Reading *Roll of Thunder, Hear My Cry*

# Reading
# *The Giver*

Pamela Loos

Philadelphia

**CHELSEA HOUSE PUBLISHERS**

VP, NEW PRODUCT DEVELOPMENT  Sally Cheney
DIRECTOR OF PRODUCTION  Kim Shinners
CREATIVE MANAGER  Takeshi Takahashi
MANUFACTURING MANAGER  Diann Grasse

**Staff for READING *THE GIVER***

EDITOR  Matt Uhler
PHOTO EDITOR  Sarah Bloom
PRODUCTION EDITOR  Bonnie Cohen
EDITORIAL ASSISTANT  Sarah Sharpless
SERIES DESIGNER  Takeshi Takahashi
COVER DESIGNER  Takeshi Takahashi
LAYOUT  EJB Publishing Services

www.chelseahouse.com

First Printing

9  8  7  6  5  4  3  2  1

Library of Congress Cataloging-in-Publication Data
Loos, Pamela.
  Reading The Giver / Pamela Loos.
    p. cm. — (The engaged reader)
  Includes bibliographical references and index.
  ISBN 0-7910-8830-8
  1. Lowry, Lois. Giver—Juvenile literature. 2. Science fiction, American—
History and criticism—Juvenile literature. I. Title. II. Series.
  PS3562.O923G5835 2005
  813'.54—dc22

                                    2005009467

# Table of Contents

1

# Contexts

WHEN WE FIRST pick up a book, we make assumptions about its contents based on its cover. When we look at the cover of *The Giver*, the strongest image is the face of the old man. His face takes up the whole length of the cover and reaches about halfway across the width, which makes the face quite prominent. His face also stands out because of its striking features: he has a very large beard and many wrinkles, making him appear quite old or like someone who has lived a tough life. The wrinkles and expression on his face also seem to show that he is very concerned or worried about something.

This feeling of something troublesome, mysterious, or unhappy is reinforced by the fact that the cover's background color is completely black. The negative feeling also comes across because the left side of the man's face is nearly completely dark and the right eye is looking as far to the side as possible. The fact that he is looking to the side gives us the feeling that he doesn't want to directly confront the troublesome thing that he is looking at or thinking about.

There is another image on the cover as well: it looks like a piece of a photograph that's been torn from somewhere else and inserted there. In this photo, there are trees and a comforting, soft sunlight. It looks like there may be snow on the ground. The image seems somewhat vacant but also positive, especially in comparison to the man's weathered face. We assume, then, that the book has some positive and negative events. Perhaps, since the man's face takes up so much of the cover, we can assume that the book is concerned with a troublesome situation for the most part but that something happens to make it better. Or the cover could be indicating that the man had led a pleasant life but something happened to make it turn bad.

Next to the man's face is the book's title. The title appears in block letters that gives it a feeling of strength. The fact

## ON YOUR OWN
### ACTIVITY #1

We said we make some assumptions about a book based on the images and other information on the cover. Imagine that before reading *The Giver* you have the opportunity to meet its author. What questions would you ask her?

that the title is *The Giver* makes us wonder if the man pictured is the one who does the giving; we also wonder what is being given. Also, how might the image of the trees tie in with the title and the man?

The man looks harsh, and since his beard is so scraggly, we might assume he lives the life of a loner. Based on the title, we might expect that he decides, or is forced, to do some act giving and, as a result, something good happens, as symbolized by the light behind the trees. Another possibility is that someone gives something to the man that brings about something good, as characterized by that same image of the trees.

When we read the back cover, we learn that a young boy named Jonas lives in a perfect world where everything is controlled. When he is 12, we're told, he is to receive special training from The Giver and will learn the truth about the pain and pleasure of life. "There is no turning back," the cover reads. From this, then, we learn that there is another character, the young Jonas, and we assume that the man on the front cover is The Giver, the one who holds all the memories, both good and bad. Now we also have some understanding of why the man on the front cover looks so weathered—he retains all memories and the truth. Apparently these are a big burden. The line "There is no turning back" piques our curiosity. Now we wonder what Jonas will find out from The Giver and how a 12-year-old boy will handle it.

There is still much more information on the book's covers. On the front, we see that the book has been awarded the Newbery Medal; on the back, we see a list of many of the other honors the book has received. When we look inside the front cover, we see several quotes from various reviews. What sort of quote taken from a review might catch the eye of a young reader? Perhaps this one: "The final flight for survival is as riveting as it is inevitable." Who wouldn't want to read something that is riveting, which means it completely holds your attention? Another reviewer calls the book "a tale fit for the most adventurous readers." Certainly, we assume, an adventurous reader would want a fascinating or exciting book, so our interest is peaked.

## ABOUT THE AUTHOR

Lois Lowry, the author of the book, has won the Newbery Medal twice. She has written many other popular books for young readers, including *Gathering Blue*, *Number the Stars*, and *A Summer to Die*. Since she's written so many titles that have become popular, we assume she must be a good writer.

Often readers are interested in knowing not just about authors' publishing information but also about their personal lives. Readers believe this may give them further insight into the books. On Lois Lowry's website, she writes, "I was a solitary child who lived in the world of books and my own vivid imagination."[1] She says she enjoyed being the middle child and being left on her own. She lived an unusual life because her father was in the military and her family

## ON YOUR OWN
### ACTIVITY #2

When we go to the library and have our choice of any book, we often look at the book's covers, both front and back, and read what's written on its back cover. What types of elements attract you to a book? Are you attracted to books on certain topics or written by certain authors? Do you like certain types of covers more than others? Why?

often moved. They lived in places as diverse as Hawaii, New York City, and Tokyo, Japan. We might think this would be a great life for someone who would later become an author; Lowry had many unusual experiences to write about and was inspired to write about a variety of settings, people, cultures, and lifestyles.

When she was 19, Lowry married a Navy officer and so continued for a time to move from place to place. She had four children, which probably helped her become good at writing books for younger audiences. She went back to school at the University of Southern Maine, where she also got her graduate degree, and then started to "write professionally, the thing I had dreamed of doing since those childhood years when I had endlessly scribbled stories and poems in notebooks."[2]

When *The Giver* was published in 1993, Lowry was in her mid-fifties and had been divorced for some time. Perhaps her divorce had her thinking about what constitutes a family, since in *The Giver* the characters believe they have figured out the best way to create families and the rules that a stable family should follow. While divorce affected Lowry personally, in the early 1990s divorce was also affecting many other Americans.

Were there other events occurring in the world around the time Lowry wrote the book that affected her writing? It may be impossible to know for sure, unless we learn this from the author herself, but we might piece together some tentative theories. In the early 1990s, the idea of being politically correct moved into the forefront. Some people were concerned that everyday terminology needed to be revised, in order to reduce or eliminate the likelihood of offending someone. For example, what once might have been called "an old person's home" might now be called a "rest home" or "retirement village." Similarly, people that previously had been referred to as "crippled" became known as "disabled" and could be categorized in a larger group of people referred to as having "special needs." As a part of this movement toward change, emphasis was placed on looking for similarities rather than differences between people. Once we read *The Giver*, we see that the whole concept of Sameness that Jonas's society comes up with can be read as an offshoot of political correctness; in the book, we see that there are positive and negative results.

In the early 1990s, as there still is today, there was an ongoing debate about abortion. Certain groups believe abortion is wrong. They believe abortion is the taking of an unborn child's life. Pro-choice groups believe that abortion should be a mother's choice since pregnancy concerns the mother's body. Similarly, euthanasia and assisted suicide have been under persistent discussion in our world, and issues related to both of these occur in *The Giver*. Once you read *The Giver*, you will see that the whole issue of the value of life is a key component to the book's society. The inhabitants no longer see all life as special. People and children are put to death for many reasons, some of which seem to be purely for convenience.

2

# Narrative Technique

AN AUTHOR'S NARRATIVE TECHNIQUE refers to how the story is told and from whose point of view. In *The Giver*, the narrator of the story writes from Jonas's perspective. We learn everything as Jonas does. The narrator also goes inside Jonas's mind and tells us what he is thinking or feeling. This type of narration is called third-person narration.

Look, for example, at the opening of the book:

> It was almost December, and Jonas was beginning to be frightened. No. Wrong word, Jonas thought. Frightened meant that deep,

sickening feeling of something terrible about to happen. Frightened was the way he had felt a year ago when an unidentified aircraft had overflown the community twice.[3]

In this passage, you see that the narrator uses phrases such as "Jonas thought" or "he had felt." When a narrator uses such words as "he," "they," or "she," it indicates that the work is written in the third person. (When an author uses "I," which is another common technique, this means that the work is written in the first person.)

In the case of *The Giver*, the work is written in the third person and from a limited point of view—that of Jonas. In other instances, a book may be written in the third person with the narrator telling us what each character, not just one character, is thinking or feeling; in this case, the narration would be termed "third-person omniscient." *Omniscient* refers to knowing everything; the third-person omniscient narrator knows everything that's happened or is happening to all the characters; this narrator knows all the characters' thoughts and feelings.

Another key element that the author uses in *The Giver* to make the reader feel it is Jonas's story is the language—the language of the story seems like what Jonas

## ON YOUR OWN
### ACTIVITY #3

Lois Lowry tells her story of *The Giver* as a third-person narrative, in this case completely through Jonas's eyes. We are inside his mind, are told his feelings, and learn about his society as he does. Explain how the story would be different if the book were still a third-person narrative but told through the eyes of another character.

would use to tell it. For example, none of the sentences are overly complex; this is what we would expect from someone who is 12 years old. Additionally, the language used is that of the inhabitants of the community. This is a society that insists on using the most exact language, but at the same time, its language is rather emotionless, as the society has come to be. The inhabitants of this community, and the narrator of this book, use "dwelling place" instead of "home" and "comfort object" to describe a child's stuffed animal, instead of "teddy bear" or some affectionate name a child might create. Parents are referred to as "father" and "mother," never as "dad" or "daddy," "mom" or "mommy."

Another narrative technique that Lowry uses to strengthen the work is the way the book is divided into chapters. Nearly every chapter is short, and many chapters cover only one significant event. This serves to make each event stand out even more. For example, the first chapter is completely focused on Jonas thinking about the Ceremony of Twelve. While other information or events are described in the chapter, nothing else is anywhere near as important or given as much attention. Similarly, when Jonas receives certain memories from The Giver, they usually are described in their own chapters or, if more than one memory is described within the same chapter, the main memory receives the most detailed description.

One chapter that stands out because of its length is the shortest chapter, which is only a little over two pages. In this chapter, The Giver gives Jonas the memory of war, which is horribly painful. At the end of the chapter, The Giver asks Jonas to forgive him for having passed the pain to him. There is no discussion about the memory of war as the two often have about other memories. This helps the author focus our attention on the memory, making its painfulness stand out even more.

Another narrative technique that affects how we read the story is that we don't become knowledgeable about certain events until Jonas does, but we are given hints about them throughout the book. *The Giver* is not a detective novel, yet the society that we're reading about is completely different from ours, meaning that there are many things about how it operates that we need to learn in order to understand the story. In a number of instances, the author gives us clues about those operations before completely explaining them.

For example, we are given some information about "release" at various times, although we don't get a full explanation until rather late in the book. At the start of the book, we are told about the pilot who mistakenly flew his airplane over the community, instilling fear in the inhabitants and causing the speaker on the public address system to command everyone to go into the nearest building immediately. Shortly after this, the Speaker tells the community that the pilot had made a mistake and that he will be

## ON YOUR OWN
### ACTIVITY #4

One of the narrative techniques that Lois Lowry uses is that she mentions certain items or events but does not immediately explain them. For example, "release" is mentioned a number of times, but only toward the end of the book do Jonas, and we the readers, find out exactly what it is. Still, readers might have been able to guess what "release" is before the total explanation is given. What information is given that might lead you to this guess?

"released." We are told that the Speaker says this almost as if it is amusing. Jonas smiles too, even though he knows that "to be released from the community was a final decision, a terrible punishment, an overwhelming statement of failure."[4]

We also get a description of how Jonas, when playing sports, had jokingly told his friend that he would be released. When the boys' coach heard this, he had "a brief and serious talk" with Jonas and made him apologize to his friend. Whereas in the first instance of release that involved the pilot there is some levity related to release, here the coach says it cannot be joked about. As the book progresses, other instances of release come up as well. For instance, Larissa mentions that a release ceremony had recently been performed at the House of the Old. Her description is quite lovely. She explains how many spoke admiringly of the older person being released. When Jonas asks her where a person really goes when released, Larissa says she doesn't know.[5] The concept, then, is not only kept secret from children but from adults, adding to our suspicions. In this case, however, the release is not done as a punishment and has positive aspects.

We find out also that Jonas and his sister believe that when people are released, they are sent to Elsewhere, another community that their own community's inhabitants have no contact with. Still, Jonas is curious to understand what is involved in release; he asks Larissa about it and later in the book asks his father about it as well. The concept of release also is hinted at when Jonas's mother explains that someone was brought before her at her job because he had broken the rules twice. She has a variety of negative responses to this and explains that, according to the rules, if the man makes another mistake he will have to be released.

Similarly, one day Jonas's father speaks of how release is handled at his job. Jonas asks for details about what his father must do when two identical twins are born and, according to the rules, one must be released. His father explains that the twins are weighed and the one to be released is prepared. "'Then I wave bye-bye,' he [Jonas's father] said, in the special sweet voice he used when he spoke to the new child." Jonas asks if someone comes to get the baby and take him to Elsewhere, and his father replies that this is the case. The situation is made light of here, shown not only through Jonas's father grinning at Gabriel as he speaks but also by Jonas's father calling Jonas by his "silly pet name" when he answers his son. This might confuse us if we are trying to guess what release really entails.

Our curiosity about release is peaked because release has been mentioned several times and Jonas, very curious himself, asks people about it. But eventually there are no more hints and we find out exactly what release entails when The Giver tells Jonas it's important that he know. Rather than transmit a memory of release to Jonas or try to explain it, The Giver has Jonas watch an actual film of a release. The film is significant because Jonas's father is in it. His father is filmed at work, and just as he's told Jonas, out of two twins he chooses the slightly smaller twin to release. Yet, rather than making the baby comfortable, Jonas's father takes out a syringe, injects the baby, and the baby dies. Father puts the baby in a box, opens a door to a chute, and puts the box in. Jonas thinks the chute looks like one they use at school for trash, which makes the death even more disturbing. Jonas's father says "bye-bye, little guy" to the baby, an overly casual remark considering the very serious circumstances.

Jonas is extremely upset. Not only was an innocent child

killed but his father did the killing. His father lied to him earlier, then, when he had explained the procedure. Also, in the film, his father hadn't looked disturbed about putting the baby to death. Think of how most young adults see their parents, or want to see them—as good, honest, and caring. Yet here Jonas sees his father in a whole other way. After seeing the film, Jonas also asks The Giver how Fiona will react when she finds out what they do when they release the elderly, since she is assigned to work in the House of the Old. But The Giver explains that just as being involved in releases doesn't truly bother Jonas's father, it won't bother Fiona, since that's what she will be taught. Once it becomes clear to Jonas what release is, he becomes determined that his society must change.

Aside from giving hints about release, Lowry also piques our interest by giving us clues when Jonas sees color. The first instance of this occurs early in the book, when Jonas is throwing an apple outside and he realizes that it changes. The change happens for just a moment, we learn, but we really have no idea of what that change is. Similarly, Jonas notices a change in the people's faces at the Ceremony of Twelve, but again he's not sure what he's seeing. Later, after he sees Fiona's hair change, he finally asks The Giver what is happening. At this point, Jonas does not even know what color is, but The Giver transmits a memory to him to help him understand. There aren't many clues to help the reader guess what Jonas is seeing. Still, the descriptions of Jonas's experiences provoke us to try and determine what he's seeing each time. We're curious and therefore pay closer attention. The fact that Jonas doesn't even know what color is and that he is excited when he notices it, shows us how different this society is from our own.

The other situation that Lowry gives us clues about is the

Ceremony of Twelve. In the beginning of the book, we're told that Jonas is quite anxious over something that is coming up, but we don't know what it is until he brings it up with his parents. We then find out that the Ceremony of Twelve is when young adults get their job assignments. Jonas has no idea of what assignment he will be given, since he feels his talents don't point to a specific role. Even though his parents assure him that the Elders are excellent at making the proper assignments, Jonas is still worried.

At the ceremony, Lowry extends the suspense about Jonas's assignment even further by having the Chief Elder skip Jonas when his turn comes to be assigned. Not only is Jonas concerned but so is the audience, so much so that the Chief Elder later apologizes. Jonas is assigned last of the whole group. Still, even after the Chief Elder finally gets to Jonas's assignment, she doesn't announce it immediately but first explains the necessary personal traits for this position. The requirements are intimidating and so Jonas is fearful. There is another disturbing factor—the Chief Elder explains that the last time the committee chose someone for this assignment, the person failed. Yet, the Chief Elder explains that she is sure Jonas meets the qualifications and that the whole community holds this job—Receiver of Memory—in the highest esteem. The crowd enthusiastically applauds and encourages Jonas, who relaxes somewhat, although he (and the readers) still doesn't know what the job entails.

To extend the suspense about Jonas's assignment even further, Lowry has Jonas arrive home and ask his parents how the committee had failed before when they made the assignment of Receiver. Jonas's parents say the name of this earlier Receiver is never to be spoken in the community and that they don't know what happened to that Receiver.

Jonas asks no more questions but instead looks inside his folder for his instructions about his new job. We expect to learn at this point what the job is but still we don't—instead of opening a big book of rules, Jonas sees that he only has a list of eight rules. One of the rules is that he not discuss his training with anyone at all, which only adds to the mystery.

Finally, when Jonas goes for his first day of training, we find out about the role of Receiver. Jonas meets The Giver, who gives him his first memory, which happens to be a good one. Only later do we learn of how horrible the memories can be. All of the mystery prior to receiving the memories only adds to our anticipation and makes the memories stand out even more.

Other information that Lowry only lets Jonas and the reader find out about in bits and pieces has to do with the previous Receiver. First we hear that the committee failed when it had chosen that Receiver. Then, Jonas's parents explain that the person's name can never be mentioned and that they do not know what happened to her. Later, The Giver explains that that Receiver had found the memories to be too much and had asked to be put to death. Apparently, the people respected the Receiver to such a degree that they did not question her decision or talk her out of it. The Giver tells Jonas how he tried not to give that Receiver, Rosemary, too many painful memories. Later, we find out that Rosemary was given to The Giver as a daughter. This intensifies the loss for The Giver and prompts him to support changing the community.

Another technique used in the narrative has to do with Jonas's friend Asher. Almost each time Asher is described, some deficiency of his is mentioned. Sometimes the flaws appear very minor, like not being able to throw the apple very well or not putting his bike in the rack as the rules require. Other times, such as when he uses the wrong words in school, the mistakes are serious enough to get him punished. Jonas is worried about what assignment Asher will be given. Even in the beginning of the book we see that Jonas has strengths, whereas Asher always appears to have many weaknesses, making Jonas's fear about Asher's assignment seem right on target.

Additionally, as the book progresses and we learn how people are punished, we wonder if Asher might become someone who is seriously punished or, since he appears to be careless, someone who becomes lost in the river. As we read the book, we have an underlying uneasiness about Asher: he is one of the few characters we know, he's Jonas's friend, and we don't want anything to happen to him. Lowry keeps showing us flaws in Asher, so we feel uncertain about him in this strict community. We pay attention to its rules even more closely and dislike it even more.

# Understanding
# the Plot

WHEN PEOPLE SPEAK about a book, frequently they refer to its plot—what happens. As you become a more experienced reader, you will find that some books don't have much plot; instead, other elements of the narrative work together to communicate the author's messages. For those books that follow the more traditional plot approach, their stories usually lead to a climax, a pivotal moment when something happens or is revealed and, as a result, circumstances for the characters change. Considering there are many options for what can happen in a climax, it may seem difficult to pick it out in a work of literature.

As you look for a climax in a book, keep in mind that almost all of the action that occurs before the climax is leading up to it. When the key event or climax happens, all of the earlier events usually fit together more clearly. They are events that were needed to help the climax occur.

In *The Giver*, what is the event that causes a significant change and sets in motion other notable events? The climax occurs when Jonas sees the film of his father putting the baby to death. As a result of this event, Jonas literally does not want to go back to his home. He is so disturbed that he stays with The Giver overnight, and this is when Jonas decides that the community must change. The Giver agrees, and the two plan how to make this happen. They decide that Jonas should leave the community, since by this action the memories he has will return to the community's inhabitants. While the people will at first suffer because of these memories, The Giver says he will help them learn how to manage the memories. If all goes well, the community will be completely transformed, realize all the riches they have been missing, and change the way their society is run.

## ON YOUR OWN
### ACTIVITY #5

Events in a work of literature often lead up to a significant event called the climax. Frequently, if some element of the plot were changed, other elements or the climax itself would be altered as well. Imagine, for example, if instead of being able to transmit memories to Gabriel, Jonas could transmit them to Fiona. How would this make life easier for Jonas? How might the escape be different?

When readers reach the climax in this book and look back at the earlier events, we see how the events were leading to this moment. For instance, early in the book, we learn that Jonas has special powers. As a result, he is given the job of Receiver of Memory. Through this experience, he meets The Giver, is guided by his wisdom, and learns from him the memories of the world at large. Then, as a result of receiving these memories, Jonas realizes what his community is missing. With each memory, his experience grows and he wants life in his community to be different.

The film that shows Jonas about release greatly disturbs him because his father is the killer and the one being killed is a baby not unlike Gabriel. In this society, both the twin in the film and Gabriel are seen as troublesome and therefore expendable. Jonas now sees his father is a killer who does not even realize how despicable it is to kill an innocent child. Jonas also sees that his father has misled him about what release really is. When Jonas realizes that Fiona, too, will be putting people to death as part of her responsibilities at the House of the Old, it is almost too much for him to bear. Jonas is angry, upset, and torn with pain. He cries and speaks sarcastically. We have never before seen Jonas act this way. These events lead him to take the courageous step of leaving.

When Jonas leaves, not only will his life never be the same but his community will be changed forever as well. It is hoped that both he and the community will be changed for the better. Jonas and The Giver realize they are taking a risk, yet when Jonas sees the film, it is as if he no longer has any choice but to leave. In a way, of course, it is like he has already left. After all, his own community has told him he must receive all memories and must not speak to anyone about them. He must go immediately home after his training each day. He is frustrated when he tries to get Asher to see color but Asher cannot do it. In short, in many ways he is already alone and outside of the community.

Jonas's life will be very different if he makes it to the real world, but even if he doesn't, he is a changed person. For example, in the beginning of the book, Jonas smiled when told about the pilot who was to be released, because he had only his own vague idea of what "release" meant. He even jokingly told Asher that he would have to be released. Yet, as the book progresses, Jonas asks other people questions about release. He is concerned about what it really is. When he finally finds out, he is driven to act, whereas earlier he had appeared content in his community.

Similarly, we see other changes in Jonas. When his father first brings Gabriel home, Jonas has no real interest in the baby. He only offers to bring Gabriel into his room at night to give his parents a break, not out of any real affection for the baby. Yet, when Jonas realizes he can actually transmit to Gabriel and later learns from his father that Gabriel will have to be released, we see that Jonas has become much more attached to the baby. Jonas even changes the plan he has made with The Giver to a more risky one in order to save Gabriel.

Additionally, there have been other signs along the way that show Jonas is changing. After he receives the war memory, for example, he is very upset to see his friends and others playing a war game and pretending to shoot each other. He is very upset that war is treated so lightly and that his friends will never understand what war really is.

We see Jonas changing as he receives more memories and learns from The Giver. For example, because of the love memory he receives, Jonas asks his parents if they love him. He is looking for reassurance from his parents that they love him. When they laugh at his question, he wonders if they really don't know what love is or if they feel they must follow the rules of their society and not acknowledge that love can exist.

Because of his experiences with The Giver, Jonas realizes that he not only wants to be loved but also wants to live life to the fullest. He throws away his pills that prevent his sexual desires. He feels much more alive as a result of this, as a result of his experiences with The Giver, and from being able to see more color. All of the memories and knowledge he gains from The Giver increase his desires and frustrations and lead to the climax of ultimate pain and anger.

Jonas is not the only one who changes because of the events in the book. The Giver changes too. First, The Giver is affected because Rosemary, the former Receiver, killed herself rather than take on all the bad memories. The Giver feels guilty for having given her those memories, even though it was his job to do so. He knows he must handle the transmissions of memory differently with Jonas. When Jonas questions why things can't be different in their society, at first The Giver has the answer but then he finally agrees to changing the community. His experiences with Rosemary and then with Jonas lead him to his decision. Without these plot elements, The Giver may never have changed or come to admit that the community needed to change as well.

Similarly, without Jonas's learning that Gabriel is to be killed, he would not have hatched his plan to leave in the middle of the night. He would not have had such an arduous journey or lacked food, since the plan was for The Giver to drive Jonas to a certain point and to have food for him. Curiously, if Jonas had not stayed the night with The Giver, Gabriel never would have been brought back to the nurturers that evening and they wouldn't have experienced his disruptive sleep and decided to release him. So, many events in the book, if they hadn't occurred or had occurred differently, could have fundamentally changed the rest of the book. In other words, the elements of the plot fit tightly together.

While an author chooses where to start a book's story and how to lead up to its climax, the author also must decide where and how to end a book. This, of course, can be pivotal. In *The Giver*, Lowry ends the book with Jonas escaping but doesn't let us know if he makes it to his ultimate destination. The reader, then, is left to decide if Jonas makes it. In making a decision, intelligent readers need to piece together a logical guess based on how the ending is described, based on prior events in the book, the book's overall tone, and what seems to be the author's intended message. By not writing a conclusive ending, the author

## ON YOUR OWN
### ACTIVITY #6

When an author doesn't tie up a book's ending neatly but expects us to reach our own conclusions, there are often hints leading us in a certain direction as to what might happen. For example, in *The Giver*, Jonas sees a waterfall, birds, and other elements of nature and is overtaken with their beauty. If the author was planning on a negative ending for her book, these elements might not have been described at all or might have been described quite differently. How might they have been negatively described? How might Jonas have been harmed by these elements?

encourages readers to think about the book even after reading the last page.

Jonas's escape with Gabriel is described in the last three
chapters of the book. Although Jonas, in order to save
Gabriel, has changed the plan from what he and The Giver
had worked out previously, initially luck appears to be on
his side: no one sees him take the food and no one sees him
escape at night on the bicycle. When the search planes fly
overhead the next morning in pursuit of Jonas and Gabriel,
Jonas is smart enough not only to quickly hide but also to
use his memories of cold to make Gabriel and himself cold,
so that the heat-sensitive equipment on the planes will not
detect their body heat. For some days the planes follow
them, and so Jonas forces himself and the baby to sleep
during the day in hidden spots while they travel at night.
Jonas knows that if they are found they will be condemned
for having disobeyed the rules of the community.

As their journey continues, there are more problems.
They run out of food and become starving and weak. They
are cold. Jonas falls off the bicycle and sprains his ankle
and cuts his knees. It rains and then at the seeming end of
the journey, it snows. Jonas is confronted with such a steep,
snowy hill that he can no longer use the bicycle.

Yet, while Jonas and Gabriel suffer from these notable
problems, there are also positive occurrences, so many and
to such a degree that they outweigh the negative events. For
example, after days of riding the bicycle, Jonas's legs are
stronger and he actually stops less to rest, which makes us
wonder if he may have other powers he doesn't know
about.

Additionally, Jonas smartly creates a makeshift net and
catches fish with it. He also recalls memories of banquets
to help rid himself of his hunger and memories of warmth

to help survive the cold. When he recalls these memories, he loses them, which means they can provide only a limited amount of help. But losing the memories is also a positive sign, since it shows that the memories are leaving him and probably returning to the community, as he and The Giver had anticipated. The escape, then, appears to be working.

Also, Jonas and Gabriel receive gifts. They see their first waterfall, birds, deer, and wildflowers. Lowry describes Jonas's reaction to what he sees as such beautiful elements of nature:

> [H]e was awed by the surprises that lay beyond each curve of the road. He slowed the bike again and again to look with wonder at wildflowers, to enjoy the throaty warble of a new bird nearby.... During his twelve years in the community, he had never felt such simple moments of exquisite happiness.[6]

Similarly, while desperately trying to make it up a hill, Jonas "began, suddenly, to feel happy. He began to recall happy times.... Memories of joy flooded through him suddenly."

As he arrives at the top of the hill, Jonas says he knows they're almost at their destination, although he is unsure how he knows this. He remembers the place, and as we learn that there is a sled "waiting for them" and that Jonas "surged with hope," we realize that this place is probably the one he had repeatedly dreamed about, the place he felt would lead him to a destination. There is a path in the snow, as if to lead them to their end point. Also, Jonas sees colored lights shining from the trees in people's homes and is reminded of the memory of love that The Giver had transmitted to him. In the last few lines of the book, Lowry says that Jonas hears singing and maybe even music coming from where he had left. Lowry writes that this could be an echo, but we know that it might be singing coming from Jonas's old community or music sent to him by The Giver.

When we think about the escape and what happens, we realize that while it is quite grueling and dangerous, there are many positive events that also occur during this time. The positives outweigh the negatives and lead us to believe that Jonas and Gabriel will make it. After Lowry points out that the families in this location are celebrating Christmas, she writes that they are waiting for Jonas and the baby. Of course, we know that Christians believe that the baby that comes at Christmas is their savior. In a way, Lowry makes us think that Jonas and Gabriel probably become saviors for their old community.

There is another technique that Lowry uses in developing her plot—foreshadowing. When authors use foreshadowing, they drop hints to their readers about what might happen later in the book. We already noted, for example, that in *The Giver* Jonas has had repeated dreams about the sled and that he feels he is destined to go to a certain place. This is a hint of what is to happen later in the book, although when we first read about the dream we may not have realized it.

Foreshadowing also occurs when Jonas reads the list of rules he must follow in his trainee position with The Giver. He wonders about the rule that says he is allowed to lie. He wonders if anyone else is allowed to lie as well. Later in the book, in fact, we find that Jonas's father hasn't told him the truth about "release." When Jonas later realizes his father has lied about this, he feels even more urgency to change his society. If his own gentle father can be involved in taking an innocent child's life, Jonas recognizes that the society has seriously altered him and probably many others as well. Another example of foreshadowing occurs when Jonas is apprehensive about the Ceremony of Twelve. In fact, while he is given a highly honored position at the ceremony, we realize as the book continues that the position is an incredible burden.

■ "I was a solitary child," said Lois Lowry, "who lived in the world of books and my own vivid imagination." She led an unusual life because her father was in the military and her family often moved. They lived in places as diverse as Hawaii, New York City, and Tokyo. Here is the young traveler in 1947.

■ Lowry has said that events in her own life made her think about the key issues in *The Giver*—particularly the themes of diversity, safety, pain, freedom, and memory. Here, Lowry is pictured with her kids in 1966.

■ Lois Lowry, a winner of two Newbery Medals, has written many popular books for young readers. She has long been interested in the concept of memory, which was part of the impetus to write *The Giver*. Lowry lives in Cambridge, Massachusetts.

■ The sled is a positive symbol in *The Giver*. When The Giver gives
Jonas his first positive memory, it's a fun sled ride down a snowy hill.
The sled occurs in a dream Jonas repeatedly experiences—he slides
down a hill, the sled stops, and he is left with a feeling that he is
heading for a place that is "good" and "welcoming." The sled also
plays a key role at the end of the book when Jonas and Gabriel
escape.

■ The isolation of the community in *The Giver* is apparent at the beginning of the book, when inhabitants are frightened as a plane flies overhead, which is not allowed. People are told by the authorities to immediately go inside their dwellings for safety. It turns out that the pilot of the plane had mistakenly flown over the community, a serious error for which he is "released."

■ In *The Giver*, the community is highly controlled. For example, cars are not allowed and people ride bicycles, presumably to cut down on accidents. When Jonas escapes from the community with Gabriel, they flee at night on a bicycle.

F

■ The society in *The Giver* seems to have the best intentions of creating a world that is safe and efficient, but most of its constraints, while seemingly not unpleasant to its inhabitants, are disturbing. For example, spouses are assigned—no one can pick a husband or wife. Similarly, children are assigned. Certain people in the community are responsible for giving birth, and these children are then given to other couples to raise, with each couple receiving two children only.

G

■ An unusual controlling element is the voice on the public address system, which apparently is heard throughout the community giving instructions. We learn that the loudspeakers don't only send out announcements but that they are listening devices as well. All inhabitants are required to keep the boxes turned on at all times.

# Characters and Characterization

WHEN WE THINK of characters, primarily we think of them as the people in a work of literature. Usually one or more characters are involved in a work; they do things and react to other characters, events, or their own thoughts. However, it is also important to realize that an author is choosing the characters—deciding how significant or insignificant the characters will be and making them seem to be simple or complex. All characters have a purpose and contribute to the work's plot, themes, and the development of other characters. As we read, we should think about why a character is in a book and what his or her function is. Sometimes, when doing this, it is helpful to think about how the work would be different if the character didn't exist.

## JONAS

In works of literature, the most important character is called the *protagonist*. In *The Giver*, Jonas is the protagonist. He appears throughout the book and, like most protagonists, is different from the other characters in the book: he does one or more things that no other character in the work does.

Jonas is 12 years old. He goes to school, lives with his family, and rides a bike, but he has a very different life than do most 12-year-olds. When *The Giver* opens, we see that Jonas's life is different, mostly because of the artificial world he lives in. But once the Ceremony of Twelve takes place, we realize that his situation is unusual not only because of where he lives but because of his own special powers. While we had been given a hint about those powers when Jonas sees the apple change, it is at the ceremony

## ON YOUR OWN
### ACTIVITY #7

In literature, a protagonist is different from the other characters, or most of them, because of his personality and beliefs. As a result, he often does things others wouldn't. Think of other books you have read or movies you've seen (*The Adventures of Huckleberry Finn* or *Spider-Man*, for example). Choose one protagonist and explain what makes him or her different. Explain the advantages and disadvantages that this character faces because of this difference.

that we are specifically told of his unique ability. The Chief Elder announces that Jonas has intelligence, integrity, courage, wisdom, and the "Capacity to See Beyond."

Of course, the ability to see beyond is the most unusual of the characteristics listed, and we learn what it entails as the book progresses: the ability to see color and to receive and transmit memories. The Giver and Jonas both have these powers. Being able to see color certainly doesn't seem very special to us, yet in the society where they live, sameness is seen as important. The idea is, for example, that if people have the same skin color, hair color, and eye color, there will be no prejudice and no one will stand out. Since clothes, houses, flower gardens, and all objects appear to be the same color, no person's possessions seem better than another's. People appear more equal, and envy and scornfulness are thereby eliminated.

What, then, is the reason for Jonas and The Giver to see color? First, it is a reminder to us not to take for granted what we have. As *The Giver* progresses, we see Jonas is fascinated the few times that he sees color, even when it happens for only a moment. Yet, when was the last time we were fascinated by color? Yes, sometimes we notice the striking color in sunsets, and when we first purchase a new item we consider color, but often we don't pay too much attention to color. Jonas's enthusiasm over color reminds us that the ability to see color is special. Additionally, as Jonas sees more color and The Giver talks to him about it, he realizes the Elders have not always made the best choices for their people. He wishes they had not put a stop to seeing color. This ability is just one of many things that inspires Jonas to think about how things could be different, and better.

More significant about the Capacity to See Beyond is that it entails giving and receiving memories. The Giver places his hands on Jonas and can transmit to him any memory. Jonas receives the memory and, as he does so, experiences it as if it were real, almost like we experience dreams when we are sleeping. What makes this different is that when Jonas stops receiving a memory, it does not go away so quickly; pain, for example, can linger for some time. When we learn that Rosemary committed suicide to avoid receiving all the painful memories from The Giver, we wonder if Jonas will be able to handle them. Yet, not only does Jonas accept the bad memories without complaint, but when he sees The Giver in pain, he tells him to transmit more bad memories so The Giver can lessen his own suffering. We realize that Jonas does indeed have courage, as the Chief Elder had pronounced.

As Jonas receives the memories and talks to The Giver about them, he learns more about the world and how it operated in other times: not only about bad things but also good, beautiful things that no longer exist. In an effort to keep their society safe, the elders have eliminated much that is bad but also much that is good, something Jonas had not suspected. Jonas realizes that the artificial society his elders have created is flawed.

The very gifts that make Jonas valuable to the community—intelligence, integrity, courage, wisdom, and the Capacity to See Beyond—are also the characteristics that make him realize he does not want to live by the rules of his society any longer. He knows that no one person should be required to take on all of society's painful memories. He has the intelligence to understand the problems and how to fix them, the integrity to stand up for what is right, and the courage to put himself at risk as he tries to escape. Not only does the ability to receive memories help Jonas realize what's wrong with his society, but his ability to transmit memories helps others as well. For example, when Gabriel cannot sleep at night and is in jeopardy of being released, Jonas transmits memories that soothe him. When Jonas tries to escape with Gabriel and the baby is cold and hungry, again Jonas transmits good memories to comfort him.

While all of Jonas's experiences with The Giver push him to realize what he must do, there is one key piece of knowledge that disturbs him to such an extent that he and The Giver make their plans for Jonas's escape. When The Giver has him see the film showing a "release," Jonas learns that release is actually not a process where a person is sent to another place but one in which the person is put to death. By learning this, Jonas realizes that his society undervalues life, that his own parents have misled him, and that his father and Fiona are willing participants in killing others for society's convenience. This information, combined with the fact that Jonas learns shortly after seeing the film that Gabriel will be released, compels him to escape and thereby try to save Gabriel's life and change the society, which will be forced to receive some of the memories he has received.

## THE GIVER

The only other character with traits similar to Jonas's is The Giver. From the way he speaks to Jonas and from his explanations of the advice he has given the Elders, we know The Giver is intelligent and wise. We see that he has integrity, since he wants what is good for the community. Also, he is willing to stay behind instead of fleeing with Jonas, so as to help the community members when Jonas's memories come flooding back to them upon his escape. We see that he has courage, since he is willing to help Jonas escape and is prepared to suffer the troubles that will ensue when the memories come back to the community members. They will be angry, but he plans to help them manage the experience. Jonas encourages The Giver to escape with him, yet The Giver feels great sympathy for the community. This sympathy is also shown when Jonas lashes out against his society's rules, angrily and with sarcasm, and The Giver is quick to explain that the community's inhabitants don't know any better.

We also see The Giver's great capacity for sympathy when he speaks of Rosemary. He explains how he tried to not give Rosemary too many painful memories at first. Then he tells how upset he was to find out that she asked to be put to death so she would not have to continue receiving any memories. He describes how, after she died, he asked to see the tape showing her injecting herself with the deadly chemicals—it was the closest he could get to being with her at death. He calls Rosemary his "daughter," and we would expect a father to have such compassion for his daughter. The Giver loved Rosemary and seems to feel guilty for inflicting so much on her, even though that was what his job required.

When examining characters in literature, it is helpful to think about how, if at all, the characters change. The Giver, for example, is more cautious when transmitting memories to Jonas, since he knows how Rosemary lost her life because of them. Also, because of Rosemary and from seeing what the painful memories do to Jonas, The Giver makes plans with Jonas for the boy's escape. While for years The Giver has been doing the duties assigned to him, he explains that the burden is incredible, since there are many horrific memories and since he is not allowed to talk to anyone about his role or the memories. The Giver is secluded and lonely as a result. His sympathies and love for Jonas inspire him to plan the escape, so that Jonas need not live this life. Also, The Giver's sympathies for all of the community mean that he will not escape himself and abandon the community members.

## ROSEMARY

Rosemary is a strong contrast to Jonas and The Giver. She is already dead when the story takes place but becomes a key reason why The Giver recognizes that the community should change. Rosemary also stands out for another reason—she, like many others in the book, most of whom are nameless, is a victim of this society's strict rules. She did not ask to be trained to become Receiver; she, like all other community members, was assigned a job. In her case, she was assigned a task highly respected by the community, yet no mechanisms were in place to help her take on this very difficult job. When Rosemary asked to be released, no one stopped her. Afterward, the authorities made it a rule that no Receiver could ever be released, but no other provisions were made to alter the position to make it less difficult.

## THE CHIEF ELDER

The Chief Elder is another key figure. She appears only in one section of the book, when she presides at the yearly ceremonies for all of the children. Her appearance shows the significance of the annual event, and the description of this event gives us a glimpse of how the community acts when together as a group. While the elder appears pleasant and appreciative, there are uneasy moments at the Ceremony of Twelve when she chides Asher for when he was very young and would confuse words and get in trouble at school. This shows that this is a society with very strict rules. The description of Asher's childhood troubles reinforces this strictness, showing that even childhood mistakes with language are not allowed. Throughout this description and all of the ceremonies, the audience is attentive and responds to the elder appropriately, reinforcing the elder's power and the people's lack of it.

## ASHER

Asher is a good friend of Jonas. Frequently, his inadequacies are mentioned. Jonas fears that there may be trouble when Asher gets his assignment at the Ceremony of Twelve, since Jonas cannot imagine what sort of position Asher can be assigned. Asher, like Rosemary, serves as a symbol of inadequacy. Neither can keep up with their society's expectations. Rosemary ends her life; as for Asher, we feel he may be punished further. In the book, very few punishments are described other than release. Throughout the book, then, we have the unpleasant sense that Asher may at some point be released. How uneasy would we feel if we were a character like Asher living in this strict community? The author wants us to examine how in our own world we treat those who do not readily fit in or who do not meet every standard of our society.

## FIONA

Another of Jonas's friends is Fiona. Jonas is attracted to her and even dreams of her. She is a caring, sensitive girl who enjoys working with the old people of the community. She, like nearly all of the community members, follows the rules; for example, she will not ask Jonas about his assignment, even though it's apparent she would like to. Fiona is an outlet for Jonas's budding sexual feelings; after he gets his assignment, her presence only reinforces for him how separated he feels from everyone, how lonely he is, and how this will only increase as he trains to become the Receiver. Fiona will be involved in putting people to death at the home for the elderly; Jonas is disturbed that, according to The Giver, she will go along with the instruction she receives. When Jonas tries to explain to Fiona and his other friends that they shouldn't play pretend war games, Fiona and the others don't understand. In short, Fiona has characteristics that make her special, but she also has characteristics of the typical inhabitant of the community. Jonas is frustrated by those typical characteristics and also by becoming more separated from her.

## OTHER CHARACTERS

Other key figures in *The Giver* are Jonas's family members. His father is a shy, quiet, and caring person. His assignment is to work in the Nurturing Center, bringing up newborn babies. At home, he also is a nurturer, calling his children pet names in an affectionate way, for example. He is willing to go out of his way for Gabriel, a child at the center that could be in trouble if he does not learn to sleep through the night and if he does not gain the proper amount of weight. However, Jonas's father does not continue to fight

## ON YOUR OWN
### ACTIVITY #8

Jonas's father's job is to bring up children for the community; his mother holds a prominent position enforcing the community's rules. This shows that gender in *The Giver* is not a main factor in deciding what job a person can have. What are the advantages to this?

for the child's well-being. Similarly, while he speaks of being distressed about possibly having to release a young twin, his father hardly seems upset in the film that Jonas sees. The film showing his father at work is what finally pushes Jonas to act.

Jonas's mother also appears to be a caring person. She and her husband take the time to talk to Jonas when he is concerned about the Ceremony of Twelve and when he has his first sexual feelings. She has "a prominent position" in the Department of Justice, where she enforces the rules of the community. One evening, she speaks of having an offender before her for the second time. She explains that she is frustrated, angry, and frightened because if he makes a mistake a third time he will have to be released. Like her husband, she is not so disturbed by the taking of life that she questions the practice or does anything to change it. She, too, is like the rest of the community, which has adjusted to all of the rules, no matter how drastic. At one point, she complains about Gabriel keeping her up at night, as if it would be a welcome relief for him to be released. Her insensitivity appears even more startling when contrasted to her husband's efforts in caring for the baby.

Lily is Jonas's young sister. She is talkative, lively, and creative. For example, when her father speaks of possibly having to release a twin, she describes to her family what might happen if one twin lived in their community and the other was released to Elsewhere. (At this point, Lily, like Jonas, doesn't know what "release" really is and believes people released are actually brought to a place called "Elsewhere.") One day, Lily says, some members of the two communities might mingle, resulting in a mix-up with the twins. When her mother makes light of Lily's story, the young girl keeps talking, asking what would happen if, in fact, there were a twin of Jonas, Lily, and their parents, all living in Elsewhere. Her father groans and tells her she must go to bed. Lily is a symbol of innocence and creativity. She imagines the different scenarios, yet her parents respond as if there is no room in their world for storytelling. Displays of imagination seem to be lost from their community as well as so much else.

Gabriel is the young infant that Jonas's family takes care of temporarily. He has distinctive light eyes, which Jonas also has, showing a connection between them. Gabriel is the only person that Jonas tries to transmit memories to that can actually receive them. Once Jonas transmits messages to the baby, he takes more of an interest in Gabriel. Additionally, as Jonas learns more from The Giver, he realizes his society's serious flaws. The fact that Gabriel can be put to death because he does not sleep through the night is another example of how this society has gone wrong, and Jonas determines to save Gabriel and do some good. Gabriel's light eyes and his ability to receive memories indicate that he has special powers as well. Jonas brings him to a new place, looking out for the next generation. Gabriel is a sign of hope, an innocent saved from the flawed community, with his whole life ahead of him.

Larissa lives at the House of the Old and is the woman Jonas bathes one day when he volunteers there. She describes to him how one of the other inhabitants was released that day in a lovely ceremony. Jonas asks her where the man went at the end of the ceremony, but she didn't know. Larissa's role in the book is to remind us that the old should not be forgotten and that old and young enjoy each other's company. She also gives the author another chance to hint at what "release" really is.

# The Function
# of Setting

IN LITERATURE, THE SETTING is where and when the story takes place. It is a key component that authors chooses to help get across their ideas. Where and when a story takes place can seriously alter its mood, characters, and events.

In *The Giver*, Jonas's story takes place in his community, although there is no explanation of where that community is located. Inhabitants use bicycles for transportation, indicating that the community is not very large and that travel outside of it is quite limited. Children from neighboring communities have visited Jonas's community, and children from his community have visited others. All apparently live in roughly the same manner, since when these visits occur no explanations appear to be needed about what is or isn't allowed.

The isolation of the community is also apparent in the beginning of the book, as inhabitants are frightened when a plane flies over their community, which is not allowed. People are told by the authorities to immediately go inside their dwellings, indicating that the plane could be danger-ous. It turns out that the pilot of the plane had mistakenly flown over the community, but this is viewed as such a seri-ous error that the voice over the community's loudspeakers announces that the pilot will be released. At this point, we do not know what "release" is, but when we find out, it makes it even more apparent how adamant the authorities are about keeping the community secluded.

We also learn that the only other time Jonas and other children see aircraft is when supplies are delivered. The delivery planes do not fly over the community but come from the west. They land on the other side of the river, out-side of the community, so children can just watch from afar. Again, this emphasizes the community's seclusion.

The plane also gives us some indication of the time period of the book. We know that it is taking place some time after planes were invented. There are only a few other clues about the time period of the book. At one point, The Giver comments that the community's genetic scientists have worked to get everyone's skin and hair color the same. This indicates the time as being in the future, since genetic engineering has not taken place to this degree as yet in our own world. Also indicating that the book takes place in the future is the fact that the weather can be controlled; many weather conditions have been eliminated to decrease prob-lems when growing food.

In summary, we do not know where or when *The Giver* takes place, but we know it is in the future. By keeping the location unknown, the author suggests that the book can take place nearly anywhere. In fact, it may take place right where we the readers live. The author may be warning us about what our own futures could be like.

While we do not know where the community is located, we know very much about how it is run and how its inhabitants live as a result, both significant elements that help define the setting. We know that elders make decisions for the community and occasionally consult with The Giver for his wisdom. There are many rules dictating behavior, and the great majority of inhabitants follow them without questioning and appear to live contentedly. The minor rule that forbids learning to ride a bicycle until a certain age is about the only rule that many inhabitants seem to break. There is joking among the inhabitants about how lengthy a process it is to change a rule, but no one seems to question any of the regulations.

A concept that is a significant component of the setting is "release," a euphemism for putting people to death. Old people live together and are cared for by people who have been assigned to work with them. Yet, they are separated from their families and are put to death seemingly arbitrarily, without their families being informed. Apparently society has decided that they have little or no value.

Another occasion when release is employed is whenever identical twins are born. The logic given for putting them to death is that it would be too confusing to have two people who look exactly alike in the same community. Those who are assigned to bring up new babies decide which of two identical twins will die, and they carry out the release. Usually one twin is smaller than the other and that is the one killed. When Jonas watches the film of his father killing a twin, his father weighs the twins and is relieved that they don't weigh exactly the same, so he will not have to decide in some other way which one will be killed. One twin, we learn, weighs two ounces less than the other. Jonas's father calls the smaller one "A *shrimp!*"—a ridiculous comment, since two ounces is an insignificant difference. The tiny difference emphasizes even further how arbitrary the killing is in this society.

Even more disturbing is the fact that babies who are born too small or don't sleep through the night are put to death. Gabriel is given extra time to reach the proper weight and sleep through the night only because Jonas's father goes before a committee and asks for this. How many other similar babies in this book have no one that stands up for them and so are killed?

The author dramatizes a point about release in the case of Gabriel. When Jonas's father explains that Gabriel will have to be released if he cannot meet certain expectations, Jonas's mother says, "Maybe it would be for the best.... the lack of sleep is awfully hard for me." Again, we are reminded of how little value is given to life. The mother's sleep is more important than a child's life. The same point is made again later. Gabriel gains the weight the leaders want him to, yet he still doesn't sleep through the night. Jonas's father explains that the night crew was "*really* frazzled" because Gabriel was so disruptive, and so it is decided he will be released. Again, someone is to be put to death merely for convenience.

There are other occasions for release in this community. One night, Jonas's mother says that someone was brought before her for committing an offense for the second time. She says she is disturbed. "The rules say that if there's a third transgression, he simply has to be released," she says. There is no flexibility in the rules: apparently, they do not change based on what the offense is or the circumstances are. Similarly, in the opening of the book, the pilot that mistakenly flies over the community will be released. This is announced to all on the public address system. Lowry writes: "There was an ironic tone to that final message, as if the Speaker found it amusing; and Jonas had smiled a little, though he knew what a grim statement it had been."[7] In this case, someone is being put to death for a mistake that caused no harm. Not only that, it is quite disturbing to the reader that the authority speaking finds this punishment amusing and that Jonas himself sees it as slightly amusing. At the beginning of the book, he, like the others, has a limited perspective of what the world can be. Keep in mind, though, that while Jonas knows release is a great disgrace, he believes the person released is taken to another community, not put to death.

The society in *The Giver* seems to have the best intentions of creating a world that is safe and efficient, but most of its constraints, while seemingly not unpleasant to its inhabitants, are disturbing to the reader. Aside from putting people to death for many reasons, the society has many other rules and controls on its inhabitants. For example, spouses are assigned; no one can pick his or her own husband or wife. Similarly, children are assigned. Certain people in the community are responsible for giving birth, and these children are then given to other couples, with each couple receiving two children only. Once the children are grown and later assigned their own spouses, they never see their parents again.

When we read about these family rules, we can see some value in them but also serious negative consequences. As

Jonas finds out, there is something wonderful about spending time with one's grandparents rather than never even knowing who they are. Also, as Jonas learns, missing from all of these families that have been controlled in so many ways is love. In our world, love is usually the reason why people get married and give birth to children and why they have family gatherings at holidays and other special occasions. The community members here do not seem to even know what love is. Jonas finds out about it from The Giver, and as soon as he does, he wishes it could exist in his own life.

When Jonas later asks his parents if they love him, they laugh in response, saying that he must use more precise language. Either they don't know what love is or they've been convinced that there is no place for it. It makes a certain amount of sense: if inhabitants are looking to make an efficient, safe community, they eliminate many problems by removing love from the equation. In this land, there will be no divorce, children will never be in trouble because they feel unloved, there will be no crimes of passion. Of course, at the same time, there also will be none of the benefits that come from love: couples will not feel drawn together by love, children and parents won't reap its benefits in their

## ON YOUR OWN
### ACTIVITY #9

The setting for *The Giver* is a community that has many rules and controls in place. Its inhabitants are trying to live in a place where there is no pain or unhappiness. Suppose, like Jonas, you lived in a community where you could only leave for brief visits to another neighboring town. How would your life be different?

daily interactions, siblings won't feel strongly toward each other.

But this society is not content to control personal relationships only by removing love. Society also curbs sexual feelings by requiring that the inhabitants take pills to stop sexual feelings and there also are rules that limit people's exposure to nudity. Additionally, all families are required to discuss their dreams with one another and, in the evening, to express their feelings. As Jonas has more meetings with The Giver, he realizes how empty these practices really are and that the feelings discussed are hardly complex, deep, or satisfying. He no longer takes his daily pill to stop his sexual desires. By doing this and working with The Giver, Jonas feels more alive and realizes what he's been missing. We the readers are also reminded of how much freedom we have.

The society in *The Giver* controls not only personal lives but also public lives. Community members do not get an education based on their skills and interests and then choose a career. Instead, these people are assigned jobs. In the interest of assigning people to positions they are most suited for, authorities follow the 11-year-olds to their volunteer jobs. Much emphasis seems to be placed on putting people in the best-suited positions. There is a belief that the authorities can do the choosing better than individuals can for themselves. Individuals have no say in the decision and they have no options to move to something else if they don't like the assignment.

Additionally, it seems rather harsh that this society forces children to do volunteer work at a young age. There is little time for playing or entertainment. Some play is mentioned, but mostly people are working or volunteering. By the age of 12, job assignments are given and the young teens start being trained after school. At home, there is no mention of watching television or doing any other relaxing activity. Homework must be done, and Jonas's mother, for example, brings work home with her to attend to in the evening. There are rules against being out in the dark.

Even seemingly small things that could pose few problems are controlled. For example, meals are delivered and leftovers picked up, which would seem to make life easier, yet this means meal times are controlled to some extent and food is not kept in homes, limiting choice and availability. Recall that when Jonas takes an apple home from his school lunch he is chastised by the authorities for what they call hoarding.

This brings up another unusual controlling element—the voice on the public address system, which apparently is heard everywhere throughout the community. The voice gives direction to the community in times of trouble, as when the plane mistakenly flew over their land. The voice also chastises individuals so that all can hear, although the individual's name might not be mentioned. This was the case when Jonas took the apple from school. The community, then, is constantly reminded of what it isn't allowed to do. We are not told how anyone in authority knew that Jonas took the apple. It may be that, just as children are followed around to their volunteer work, there are people who are responsible for watching and following people in other circumstances. We also learn later that the loudspeakers don't only send out announcements but that they are listening devices as well. All inhabitants are required to keep the boxes turned on at all times. Jonas is shocked when he learns that The Giver has the authority to turn off his box.

There are also no animals in *The Giver* except for children's "comfort objects," the soft stuffed animals they take to bed with them. What is to be gained by this? Since children and people are so busy, they apparently shouldn't be distracted by pets; additionally, pets can turn on people and harm them or fight with each other. Of course, then, no one in this community gets the many benefits of pets or of being able to raise animals to make food or other supplies. There are not even any wild animals that people might enjoy.

The society has removed some clear problems: there is no bad weather, which removes problems for those growing crops, and there are no hills, making it easier to travel. While these benefits are obvious, nevertheless there are losses associated with each of these things. For example, when Jonas receives the sleigh-riding memory, we realize that such an activity is impossible without snow and without hills.

Another example of something eliminated that seems to be clearly beneficial is that when someone gets hurt, he or she is administered pain medication that stops the pain immediately. How could this not be good? When Jonas meets with The Giver, we realize there is a value in pain. Pain teaches us to avoid making mistakes and to take care when we make decisions. The book focuses on this issue of the elimination of pain. The whole idea of the position of Receiver is that this person will preserve humanity's memories, withstand the burden of all horrific memories, so that everyone else will not have to experience pain. This has made The Giver's life nearly impossible to live and leaves the non-pained individual helpless when making decisions or in need of wisdom.

Language is also controlled in this society, both in public and private instances. For example, Asher is made fun of for using the wrong words as a child, Jonas corrects his own use of a word that he's only thinking about, and his parents correct him when Jonas asks about love. People are required to apologize when they make a mistake, and they almost always use the same language when they do so, as does the person responding to their apology. The result of this insistence on using certain language is that people are saying words by rote rather than sincerely making their own responses. The insistence on precise language is so orchestrated that it has made language empty.

In summary, the setting of *The Giver* is in the future in a highly controlled land, a land that could develop out of the place we readers live in today. While this community is structured to make it ideal, a utopia, the excessive rules, lack of freedom, lovelessness, and lack of individuality actually make it far from ideal. Since its inhabitants don't know of any other way of life, they live their days seemingly contented. Only after Jonas becomes educated and dissatisfied with his way of life does change for the community become possible. Lowry is showing us the many problems that can develop in such a controlled society and warning us to never lose our curiosity, knowledge, and depth, lest we end up in such a society ourselves.

## ON YOUR OWN
### ACTIVITY #10

In Lois Lowry's book The Giver is the only person with painful memories. Yet, Lowry makes the point that living in a place where there is no pain or no painful memories is not good for the inhabitants and causes other problems. Interview an adult about a painful memory that they have. Ask them to explain the positives and negatives of having this memory.

# Understanding
# Themes and Symbols

IN WORKS OF ART, a theme is an idea that the work is presenting; in literature in particular, a theme can be seen as a message that the author is sending to the readers. There may be one key theme that the author is presenting, yet frequently there is more than one.

How do we determine what the themes are when we read a book? To figure them out, we need to ask ourselves why we think the author wrote the work, what the author wants us to think about as we read. Lowry prompts her readers to think about a number of issues. In *The Giver*, an artificial society

48

exists and its inhabitants have done many things to make this society pain-free. Ask yourself if you would like to live in a world where there is no pain. The answer rather clearly is, "Yes, of course." Yet, Lowry's story shows that while a pain-free world sounds great, it ends up causing problems that we really would not want at all.

More specifically, the job of Receiver, which Jonas is being prepared for, is to preserve the memories of all pain, so that others need not be burdened by them and also so that the wisdom learned from the pain is not completely forgotten. This results in two key problems. The first problem is that the Receiver must live a secluded life, unable to share most of what he knows and required to bear the burden of enormous pain. The job of Receiver, then, is an incredible burden, as evidenced by Rosemary killing herself while in training. If the person who has the job of Receiver can manage it, his life will be almost unbearable; if the Receiver cannot manage it, the society is in serious jeopardy, since the pain would revert back to the inhabitants if there were no Receiver. The second key problem with the Receiver's role is that members of society have no memories of pain and, therefore, when decisions are to be made, they either struggle over them for long periods or they go to the Receiver for advice. When it comes to decision-making, then, the inhabitants of this artificial world are nearly helpless. The Receiver is the only person with wisdom, which he has gained through remembering all of history's mistakes and horrors as well as from good memories of events and things that no longer exist in the highly structured society.

This is a good place to start thinking about themes, since *The Giver* is the title of the book, which clearly indicates that the author wants us to think about The Giver, who is training Jonas to become the new Receiver. No matter what the person is called who holds all of the inhabitants' memories, Lowry wants us to think about this character's role. Clearly, we realize that the book contains a theme about pain. First, no matter how hard we may try, it is impossible to completely remove pain from life. Plus, pain brings wisdom, a key trait for all responsible, contributing members of society to have and something that makes it possible for society to progress.

Aside from the memories that The Giver transmits to Jonas, does pain exist in any other form in this book? Is any other pain described? Think of the very end of the book. At the end, we have a long description of Jonas escaping with Gabriel. What pains do they suffer? Jonas is afraid they may be caught, and he knows that if they are caught, they will be put to death. Also, both are very cold and hungry.

How do they manage to combat the pain? Jonas is determined that life will be better for him, Gabriel, and all the others they left behind if he leaves and the memories return to the people. He is completely focused on achieving the

## ON YOUR OWN
### ACTIVITY #11

In *The Giver*, people have no painful memories and so they go to The Giver for help and wisdom when important decisions are to be made. The book points out some themes regarding memory—for example, that there is a value in bad memories, since we often learn from our own mistakes and the mistakes of others. Describe a situation where you made a mistake. What lesson did you learn from the situation? How will you handle a similar situation in the future as a result?

goal. Additionally, Jonas uses his own resourcefulness to make sure they sleep at the best times and find food to eat. He also uses his good memories to comfort them and bring them warmth. This ending, then, shows that the author has more to say about pain—that pain can be diminished and overcome by good memories and by staying focused on a better future and doing everything possible to get to that better place. By the end of the book, Jonas has received many painful memories from The Giver and realized he could still survive; he has been made aware of his own strength of will. There is another message about pain, then—that while it temporarily weakens us, it ultimately can make us stronger.

Aside from ideas about pain, *The Giver* has other themes. Just as the society in the book has tried to control pain, it controls many other things in an effort to make its world as risk-free, trouble-free, and seemingly effective as possible. Aside from the role of The Giver, there are many other things in this society that are very different from the society we live in. There is one thing in particular that is described in numerous ways throughout the book—release. The concept of release appears in the very first chapter, when talking about the pilot who mistakenly flew a plane over the community. As the book progresses, we are not told specifically what release means but are given more examples of it. We learn, for instance, that release is used on old people, on babies that are twins or babies who don't sleep through the night, and on repeat criminals. We also learn that Rosemary had requested it.

We are not told what release specifically is until quite late in the book, although we may have figured it out before that point. In this society, release—which we find out is putting people to death—is used to make the society run more effectively. The people in this society believe the elderly have no use, so they are made to live together so they won't burden their families, and then they are killed. Repeat criminals, rather than being rehabilitated, are also killed. As we learn of other reasons for killings, we see how in this society life has lost much of its value. The pilot who made a mistake of flying his plane over the wrong area will be released. When twins are born, one is released because, the inhabitants believe, it would be too confusing to have two people that look the same. Similarly, Gabriel is to be released because he doesn't sleep through the night.

What is the author's message about life? In our society today, different groups fight either for or against abortion, for or against allowing someone who is in a vegetative state to be allowed to die, for or against executing people who have been found guilty of capital crimes. But Lowry seems to be telling her readers that if you start to believe you can take life for certain reasons, it may be very easy for more reasons to be accepted. She warns us that life cannot be eliminated for our own convenience.

What else is different about this world Lowry has created and therefore may be indicating other themes? Think about the rules in this society and what they mean for the people living there. For example, people apply for a spouse and are appointed one by the authorities. Also, only certain people have children and those children are given to parents, with each set of parents having no more than two children. Once the children are old enough to move out and have their own families, they never see their parents again. The parents, then, never see any grandchildren, and these children don't know who their grandparents are. Another rule is that no one can choose a career:

children do volunteer work from a young age so the authorities may find out what they are good at; then, at only 12 years old, they are assigned a job to be trained in and start their careers.

The goal of these rules is to create a pleasant, risk-free, efficient society. The rules seem to work well, but we wonder if these people can truly be happy. For example, in our society, great emphasis is put on the choice of a mate; at the same time, people are now able to divorce if their marriages don't work out. In other societies today, people are still assigned mates, yet for most Americans this seems unthinkable. Similarly, parents are in control of how many children they have or don't have and can even adopt children. Most children know who their grandparents and other relatives are. In regard to careers, most teenagers start thinking of possible careers based on their strengths and what they enjoy doing. People also can choose a career and then switch to a different one.

While most people in *The Giver* seem content to follow the rules, and while the society seems to be functioning effectively, as we read we begin to question the benefits and losses that occur because of the rules. As the book progresses, Jonas himself questions a number of the rules as well. For example, Jonas finds out from The Giver what love is. As a result, he realizes how much better his world could be if love still existed, if families complete with grandparents could celebrate around a warm fireplace with pets and presents and experience this full, deep emotion. He questions why the old are pushed away from everyone else and why people can't have pets or express strong feelings for each other.

We realize that Lowry wants us to think about a theme involving freedom and risk. Yes, a person might pick the wrong person to marry; yes, children might not always get along so well with their parents or grandparents; and yes, people could get bitten and hurt by pets. Yet, Jonas and the reader realize that even with all of these possibilities for mistakes, overall people still have a better chance of being truly, deeply happy if they can make their own choices and love their families and friends completely. Lowry is showing us the importance of freedom and the importance of being able to live as complete human beings, experiencing our full potential in feelings such as love and happiness.

How else is the society in *The Giver* a very different one from what we are used to? Many rules are created and followed so that there is a sameness and lack of individuality. Specifically, at each age, children are only allowed to do certain things, wear certain clothes, and have their hair cut a certain way. Curiously, there is no color, so that there are no apparent differences based on skin color, hair color, or any other color choices that may occur—whether in clothing, bicycles, homes, gardens, etc. Similarly, if there is no color, the sky is not more or less blue, a sunset more or less saturated. Each day is like the others; people and places appear more similar. Yet, Jonas says he would like to pick

## ON YOUR OWN
### ACTIVITY #12

Lois Lowry is also advocating the theme that freedom of expression is important. Jonas voices this idea when he wishes he could choose what he wears each day. Think of ways that we express individuality in our own society. Describe some of these and explain their advantages and disadvantages.

the color of his tunic when he gets dressed in the morning; he is thrilled to see the red of a bright apple or of Fiona's hair. The lack of individuality in this world makes us see another theme—that freedom of expression is valuable and, by having it, people develop new ideas and creations.

Aside from themes, works of literature frequently use symbols or symbolism. A symbol is something that stands for something else, and a symbolic action is something that is done to indicate something else. For example, a country's flag is a symbol of the country itself. When people salute the flag, the flag stands for their country and they are showing that they honor their country. Similarly, when people burn a flag, it shows their disagreement with and strong negativity toward that country's policies, leaders, or people.

In *The Giver*, we can see various symbols. How do we know when something is being used as a symbol? Sometimes we realize it because it is a detail that the author makes a point of drawing our attention to. For example, this occurs in *The Giver* when we read the author's description of Gabriel's light eyes. We learn that Jonas also has light eyes, as does The Giver. The light eyes connect these three characters.

As we read the book, we see that the eyes are just one sign of a connection between these characters. All three of them have special abilities. In the case of The Giver and Jonas, they can see color and transfer memories. Gabriel is the only person Jonas tries to transfer memories to that is able to receive them. We can say, then, that the light eyes are a symbol of special powers: the eyes are so light that more can be brought in through them; they indicate the person's ability to see more than the other characters. Not only can Jonas and The Giver see all of the past, they also can see what's wrong with the present and what needs to be done to make it better.

This idea of the strength in light and brightness is also carried through symbolically in the apple, Fiona's hair, and the fireplace and lights in the love memory. All of these bright objects also symbolize a better world. The apple is the first object Jonas sees in color, representing a step toward his realization that the world can be different. The red in his friend's hair indicates that she too may be special. We know if Fiona is Jonas's friend that there probably is something different about her. We learn that she is very sensitive toward the old people and toward Jonas. Her hair color, like the apple's color, is another indication that the world need not be so bland and lacking in individuality. Similarly, the fireplace and lights are another symbol of brightness and hope for a better world. The fireplace occurs in the memory of love, the strongest positive memory The Giver passes on to Jonas, and because of it Jonas desires a deeper and better life for all. Lightness and brightness, then, are symbolic of special powers and a better future.

Similarly, the sled is a positive symbol. When The Giver gives Jonas his first positive memory, it's a fun sleigh ride down a snowy hill. Not only did Jonas not know, prior to this, what a sled is, but he also had never seen snow or a hill. The experience shows that he has special powers to receive the people's memories and that he has missed out on the simple pleasures that we, the readers, know about but that no one in Jonas's world has experienced. It marks the beginning of his learning about how the world can be a better place.

The sled also occurs in a dream Jonas repeatedly experiences. In the dream, he slides down a snowy hill, the sled stops, and he is left with a feeling that there is some place he still has to reach, a place that is "good," "welcoming," and "significant." The sled also plays a key role at the very end of the book when Jonas is trying to escape. At this point, Jonas is near his breaking point, having struggled through terrible cold without enough food and in fear of being captured and put to death; at the same time, he must be responsible for Gabriel. As he climbs a snowy hill, he feels that the place is somehow familiar, "a memory of his own." We think it may remind him of his dream, which perhaps was actually a premonition of this moment. He and Gabriel get on the sled and head toward lights, where people are waiting for them, celebrating. The sled, then, is symbolic of a new and better life.

Hills are also symbolic. In the book, we are told that there are no hills in this society. Yet, in the memory with the sled, the hill is only positive. Jonas does not have to climb it but can just enjoy going down it on the sled. At the very end of the book, he must climb the hill, but when he reaches its flat top, he realizes the sled will zoom him down, seemingly into a new and better life for all. The hill, then, is like much of life—it has a hard part and an easy part, but having it to conquer certainly makes life fuller.

# Afterword

WHEN WE LOOKED at the cover of *The Giver* for the first time, before we knew what it was about, we made some assumptions about the book's contents. After reading the book, the cover may seem to have a different significance. For example, we now know that The Giver, pictured on the cover, is in fact a very sensitive and kind man. Yet before reading, because of the harshness of the face that appears on the cover, we perhaps were tempted to believe differently. We also realize that The Giver is a very giving person, not only because he literally gives Jonas memories but because he is willing to help Jonas escape while he himself stays behind to help the community through the trauma of adjusting to their new memories.

Another element on the cover is the patch of trees with pleasant sun and perhaps snow on the ground. If we look at the image more carefully, we see that more trees are in the background as well. The trees that are further away make us wonder what is beyond them, just as Jonas wonders about Elsewhere, the place beyond his home community. Through most of the book, Jonas thinks that Elsewhere is just another community where the people who are released must live the rest of their lives. Later, he finds out that when people are released, they are actually put to death. In speaking with The Giver, Jonas learns that there still is an Elsewhere, but that people living there don't live the way they do in his community—they live more fully.

Before we had read *The Giver*, we didn't know that the image with the trees would specifically relate to something in the story. Now, we realize that the image with the trees and snow refers to a few things. First, Jonas, having lived in a protected world his whole life, didn't know what snow was and or about the fun of sledding. This was the first positive image The Giver transmitted to him. At the very end of the book, when Jonas and Gabriel are exhausted, cold, and starving, it starts to snow. Yet, Jonas is so positive about reaching their destination that rather than see the snow as another problem, he comments on its beauty. Ultimately, the snow also makes it easier for the two to reach their destination, since when they reach the top of the hill, a sled is there for traveling over the snow. Additionally, Lowry tells us there is an incision in the snow, as if it is leading the two weary travelers to their goal.

The fact that there is a soft, golden light in the cover image is also significant, not only because the light is inviting but because in the book light has positive connotations. For instance, it indicates specialness—Jonas and Gabriel have light-colored eyes and both are different from the rest of the community, with unusual powers. Also, in the strongest image The Giver passes on to Jonas, the scene of a loving family at Christmas, the lights twinkle on the tree and a warm light emanates from the fireplace. At the end of the book, Jonas sees the same lights ahead of him as he nears his destination.

After reading the book, we recognize the significance of the cover image of The Giver being in black and white, while the image of the trees has color. The Giver lives in a community where only black and white exist, although some people, such as himself and Jonas, can see color. As the book progresses, Jonas sees more color and the new place he approaches at the end has trees decorated in colored lights.

Winter is often seen as the season one must go through to get to spring: deadness and cold are necessary steps before new life sprouts. It seems fitting, then, that Jonas would have to travel a wintery path to make it to his new life. Once there, we assume, everything will be so much more enriching and fulfilling, and Jonas will be starting anew in a loving environment, more conducive to his well-being.

Before reading *The Giver*, we also read the back cover, where we were warned that Jonas would receive the truth and that there would be "no turning back." We now realize that Jonas cannot turn back because he literally cannot return to his community. After finding out the truth, Jonas puts his life on the line, even though he is still a teenager. The book, therefore, may have turned out to be even more suspenseful and gripping than we had expected.

Are there other books like *The Giver* in which a society is highly controlled in an attempt to eliminate trouble and approach perfection? In fact, throughout history people have been fascinated with the idea of a perfect place. As mentioned earlier, such a place is referred to as a "utopia." A synonym for utopia is "Shangri-la." This also refers to a place that approaches perfection, a place that is also remote and beautiful. Shangri-la was originally the name of a place in a popular novel by James Hilton, *Lost Horizon*, which was published in 1933 and later made into a movie.

According to the story, Westerners looking to escape from war in Central Asia are taken on a plane, only to crash somewhere near a remote community in the Himalayan Mountains. This place is untouched by modernism, materialism, violence, crime, and hunger. People live connected to the environment and do not age at the usual pace. The travelers who have crashed here are told that they will have to wait a while to get out, since outsiders who could help them only come through infrequently. As time goes on, the travelers ask about leaving and are always given cryptic sorts of answers. For the small group of Westerners, some accept the situation but one does not. One ambitious man feels trapped like a convict and is willing to go to great lengths, even risking his own life, to escape. What is curious in *Lost Horizon* are the very different reactions to the situation: some people are content with it, yet another must fight it with all his power.

This brings to light another issue about utopia. Since we all are so different, wouldn't utopia mean something unique to each of us? In light of this, wouldn't it be nearly impossible to try to create a utopia?

In real life, people have also tried to create their own utopian societies. Louisa May Alcott, the author of *Little*

*Women*, lived for a time with her family in a structured community, as did a certain number of other Americans in the early nineteenth century. At other points in history, people have formed communes, where inhabitants live close to the land, responsibilities are shared, and there is little contact with the outside. Rules were in place to keep the communities peaceful and effective.

The 1960s also were a time when people rebelled against society and searched for new alternatives. Today, some people look back at the time immediately before the 1960s as idyllic because it appeared simpler and seemingly less problematic. In the 1998 movie *Pleasantville*, this notion of the 1950s as an untroubled, easier time is turned on its head. Two teens from the 1990s wind up in Pleasantville, a town based on the town in one teen's favorite television show. Everything appears fine in Pleasantville—the high school basketball team makes every shot; nothing ever catches on fire, so the firemen actually do help get cats out of trees; and wholesome family values seem to be the norm.

But on closer examination, there are problems in the

## ON YOUR OWN
### ACTIVITY #13

Throughout history, people have thought about how to create a perfect world, a utopia. In works of art, however, utopian societies usually turn out to have flaws, often very serious ones. In the real world, for many students, part of a perfect life would be not going to school or not having to keep their bedrooms clean. Imagine that such things could actually happen. What would be the positive and negative consequences?

town of Pleasantville. All of the books in the town's library are blank. There appears to be no real passion. A character flipping hamburgers in the local soda shop actually longs to be an artist but, as in Jonas's world, there is no color here. As the movie progresses, the two teens change the Pleasantville world, opening it up to a range of possibilities, yet provoking an intense backlash from the conservative townspeople, who see the change as dangerous. The inhabitants are awakened to a world of color, passion, books, and art, yet, at least initially, there is a price to be paid for the change.

A world that appears pristine and happy but lacks freedom and self-expression is also presented in *The Truman Show*. In this 1998 film, the main character has a life that seems perfect—a good job, a nice wife, and a home in a neat, sunny town. Yet his "life," although he doesn't know it, is completely staged for a television show, taking place in an enormous movie studio, where everyone but the main character is acting a part. His whole life has been filmed in a completely phony world, and he finally catches on when some slip-ups occur on the set. Ultimately, he escapes so he can live his own life—no matter what troubles may occur, at least they will be real.

When Lois Lowry made her speech upon receiving the Newbery Medal for *The Giver*, she talked about the events in her own life that made her think about the key issues in her book—diversity, safety, pain, freedom, and memory.[8] She, like Jonas, craved freedom and diversity as a young girl living in Japan because of her father's military responsibilities. The family lived in a gated community that was sheltered and very American. The young Lowry would sneak outside and revel in the people and activity, so vibrant and exciting. Once, a woman walked up to her and said something in Japanese and Lowry pulled away. A few moments later, Lowry realized the woman had given her a compliment, but it was too late for Lowry to attempt to thank her. Years later, when Lowry asked her mother why they had lived in this community rather than among the Japanese people, her mother was rather surprised by the question and said she had found it comfortable.

The issues of comfort and safety brought on by people remaining sheltered and following rules also came up in Lowry's life in college. She lived with a number of other bright young women, who she described as dressing the same, doing the same activities, even knitting the same style of argyle socks for their boyfriends. One woman who was smart but acted different from the group in a number of ways was excluded by the group, an action that Lowry says must have made them feel safer although it was harmful.

The thoughts about painful memories came to Lowry at different points in her life as well. In one instance, she remembers her father in a nursing home, commenting that he doesn't remember what happened to his one daughter. The daughter had died at a young age, but at that moment

## ON YOUR OWN
### ACTIVITY #14

In *The Giver*, the community is highly controlled. For example, cars are not allowed and people ride bicycles, presumably to cut down on accidents. Similarly, people are not permitted to be out after dark, perhaps to reduce the possibility of crime. Look at your own life and think of some of the rules or laws that limit your freedom. Explain how they curb your freedom but also explain their benefits, either for you or society.

he had forgotten. Perhaps this could seem like a good forgetting, since it seems fair for an old man to be spared some of his most painful memories. Yet, Lowry questioned that logic and filed the memory away for her writing.

Similarly, Lowry thought about painful memory when she was speaking before an audience about *Number the Stars*, her novel about two young girls living at the time of the Holocaust. A young woman in the audience asked why the story of the Holocaust still needed to be retold. Lowry later thought about the question and about her own German daughter-in-law, who had insisted that the story be repeated often. In this instance and in her father's comment about his own daughter, Lowry believed forgetting was safer and easier but knew it really wasn't better.

In *The Giver*, Lowry pays a great deal of attention to the memories that The Giver has and transmits to Jonas. Emphasizing this fact is that Lowry titles her book *The Giver*. But since the community honors the Receiver of Memory and since Jonas, the protagonist, is being trained to be the new Receiver, it would seem logical, actually, to have called the book "The Receiver." Why didn't Lowry call it that? While there are many books that have straightforward titles, those that don't should make us contemplate why the authors chose the titles they did.

In *The Giver*, receiving can be viewed as a rather passive action, but Jonas is seldom passive when he receives a memory. He asks questions and thinks about the memory when he goes home. Also, the community gives the title of Receiver to the person who holds all the memories, but perhaps this name isn't exactly correct. For example, once the Receiver receives all the memories, which occurs in his training, no more receiving takes place. The Receiver must then give advice only when asked and handle the memories on his own. Remembering and managing the memories means that the Receiver does not have a normal life; he is really a martyr, someone who has given up his life for the sake of the community.

As the book nears its end, we see another way that Jonas is more of a giver than a receiver—he risks his life to save Gabriel and the community. In the same way, The Giver may be giving his life too, for he truly doesn't know how the inhabitants will respond when the memories come flooding back to them. He is willing to endure their wrath for the sake of great improvement, but if the plan doesn't work, his life will be in jeopardy.

*A Summer to Die* (1977)

*Find a Stranger, Say Goodbye* (1978)

*Anastasia Krupnik* (1979)

*Autumn Street* (1979)

*Anastasia Again!* (1981)

*Anastasia at Your Service* (1982)

*Taking Care of Terrific* (1983)

*Anastasia Ask Your Analyst* (1984)

*Us and Uncle Fraud* (1984)

*The One Hundredth Thing About Caroline* (1985)

*Anastasia on Her Own* (1985)

*Switcharound* (1985)

*Anastasia Has the Answers* (1986)

*Rabble Starkey* (1987)

*Anastasia's Chosen Career* (1987)

*All About Sam* (1988)

*Number the Stars* (1989)

*Your Move J.P.!* (1990)

*Anastasia at This Address* (1991)

*Attaboy, Sam!* (1992)

*The Giver* (1993)

*Anastasia, Absolutely* (1995)

*See You Around Sam!* (1996)

*Stay! Keeper's Story* (1997)

*Looking Back* (1998)

*Zooman Sam* (1999)

*Gathering Blue* (2000)

*Gooney Bird Greene* (2002)

*The Silent Boy* (2003)

*Messenger* (2004)

1   Lois Lowry—Author. *www.loislowry.com/bio.html.*

2.  Ibid.

3.  Lois Lowry. *The Giver*. New York: Laurel-Leaf Books, 1993, p. 1.

4.  Ibid., p. 3.

5.  Ibid., pp. 31–32.

6.  Ibid., p. 171.

7.  Ibid., p. 2.

8.  Lois Lowry. Newbery Acceptance Speech. *www.loislowry.com/pdf/ Newbery_Award.pdf.*

Lowry, Lois. *The Giver*. New York: Laurel-Leaf Books, 1993.

Madden, Caolan. *SparkNote on* The Giver. New York: Spark Publishing, 2005. *www.sparknotes.com/lit/giver/*.

Layne, Steven L. *This Side of Paradise*. St. Charles, IL: North Star Books, 2001. A boy's father forces his family to move to a supposed paradise that the father's company, Eden Corporation, controls. The boy unearths the horrible secrets that make this sick utopia possible.

Lowry, Lois. *Gathering Blue*. New York: Laurel-Leaf Books, 2002. A companion volume to *The Giver*, here the society is behind the times and also full of greed, cruelty, envy, and anger, a result of strict rules enforced by those above. A young woman artist may be the key to change.

Lowry, Lois. *Messenger*. New York: Houghton Mifflin/Walter Lorraine Books, 2004. This book includes Jonas, now leader of the utopian society that he entered as a young boy in *The Giver*. The society, however, is closing itself off to outsiders, something that had previously been unthinkable. Another young boy with special powers may be its savior.

Marsden, John. *Tomorrow, When the War Began*. New York: Laurel-Leaf Books, 1996. In this book, teenagers are in trouble not because of a forced utopia but because they've returned from a camping trip only to find their world turned upside down. Their country has been invaded and all its citizens made prisoners. Can life as the teenagers knew it be restored?

Stephens, J.B. *The Big Empty*. New York: Razorbill, 2004. In this book, teenagers are involved in creating a new world. In the one they lived in, three-quarters of the inhabitants have been killed by a deadly virus.

Whelan, Gloria. *Fruitlands: Louisa May Alcott Made Perfect*. New York: HarperCollins, 2002. This novel is based on journals written by a real young girl who's father moved his family to an experimental commune that was to be a place of peace and communing with nature. The young girl is Louisa May Alcott, who grew up to become the famous author of *Little Women*.

**PAMELA LOOS** has written and/or researched more than 40 books about literature, covering a range of authors and works. She is a certified English teacher.